The Best Parts of CHRISTMAS

Bethanie Deeney Murguia

Candlewick Press

Today is Christmas Tree Day,
and Fritz has found the very best tree.
“This one! This one!” he calls.

It's a *real* tree! A *whole* tree!
And it will be coming *inside* Fritz's house.

Mama and Papa are breaking house rule number five:
no branches, sticks, or twigs allowed indoors.
But Fritz doesn't remind them.

He is in charge of ornaments—
the most important job.

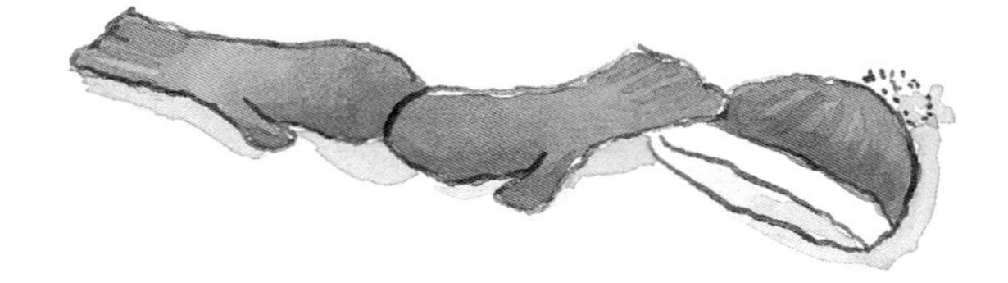

Mama says, “Be sure to spread them out,”
but Fritz knows the ornaments want
to be close to their friends.

He surveys his work. If only there were more ornaments . . .

Then Fritz makes an amazing discovery—
almost anything can be an ornament!

His tree is like a magnet for good things.
First ornaments. Then candy canes
and gingerbread cookies.

And presents! Day by day, gifts appear.
Fritz arranges, rearranges, and gently shakes each one
as the family gathers on Christmas Eve.

The best parts of Christmas Day
happen around Fritz's tree.

At night, Fritz leans in close and makes a wish.
He wishes it could always be Christmas.

In the days that follow, Fritz's tree listens when he reads and stays quiet while he naps.

But before long, Fritz's tree is almost bare.
"Time to take the tree away," says Papa.
"It will help new trees to grow," says Mama.

Fritz is *not* ready for Christmas to be over.

If only he had some ornaments . . .

And then Fritz remembers—
almost anything can be an ornament.

For cookie bakers, ornament makers, and everyone who believes in the magic of Christmas

First edition 2015

Library of Congress Catalog Card Number 2014949720
ISBN 978-0-7636-7556-1

15 16 17 18 19 20 CCP 10 9 8 7 6 5 4 3 2 1

Printed in Shenzhen, Guangdong, China

This book was typeset in Caecilia Roman.
The illustrations were done in pen and ink and watercolor.

Candlewick Press
99 Dover Street
Somerville, Massachusetts 02144

visit us at www.candlewick.com